PUFFIN BOOKS

The Last Castaways

Roo lives with Harry Horse and Mandy in an old farmhouse in the Scottish Borders. She has turned down several film offers since the publication of *The Last Polar Bears*, preferring instead to concentrate on rabbits. It is her ambition to own one eventually. She is currently working on her first book, provisionally entitled *The Bad Rabbits.*

Harry Horse writes and illustrates children's books. His titles include *The Last Gold Diggers,* for which he won the Smarties Gold Award. He is well known as a political cartoonist and has produced cartoons for the *New Yorker*, the *Guardian* and the *Sunday Herald.* Unusually, rabbits do not play a large part in his life.

Poopy is a small grey plastic walrus who lives in Roo's basket. He has no hobbies, but likes to lurk on the stairs, waiting to trip people up. This is his first (and hopefully his last) book.

Some other books by Harry Horse

THE LAST POLAR BEARS
THE LAST GOLD DIGGERS
THE LAST COWBOYS

The Last Castaways

Being, as it were,
an Account of a Small Dog's
Adventures at Sea

Written and illustrated by Harry Horse

PUFFIN BOOKS

PUFFIN BOOKS

Published by the Penguin Group
Penguin Books Ltd, 80 Strand, London WC2R 0RL, England
Penguin Putnam Inc., 375 Hudson Street, New York, New York 10014, USA
Penguin Books Australia Ltd, 250 Camberwell Road, Camberwell,
Victoria 3124, Australia
Penguin Books Canada Ltd, 10 Alcorn Avenue, Toronto, Ontario, Canada M4V 3B2
Penguin Books India (P) Ltd, 11 Community Centre, Panchsheel Park,
New Delhi – 110 017, India
Penguin Books (NZ) Ltd, Cnr Rosedale and Airborne Roads,
Albany, Auckland, New Zealand
Penguin Books (South Africa) (Pty) Ltd, 24 Sturdee Avenue,
Rosebank 2196, South Africa

Penguin Books Ltd, Registered Offices: 80 Strand, London WC2R 0RL, England

www.penguin.com

First published 2003
9

Typeset in 13/15 American Typewriter and 12/15 Bookman

Made and printed in England by Clays Ltd, St Ives plc

British Library Cataloguing in Publication Data
A CIP catalogue record for this book is available from the British Library

ISBN 0–141–31461–3

For Mandy and Roo

Author's Note:

I should like to make it clear that Roo's reputation has in no way been damaged by the following story. My version contains no facts that are not true. Roo is not good on sand, snow or sea.

I think that the evidence speaks for itself. If Roo wishes to proceed with her version, then so be it.

witnessed by: ~~Arthur Grumble~~   signed: H.A.
                    solicitor

Dear Child,

Roo and I are both well. I have been pottering around in the garden and Roo has been helping me. She's not really a gardening type of dog, unless you count digging large holes in the lawn as helping, which I don't.

To distract Roo from digging another big hole by the pond, I took her to the Dog Show at the community hall on Sunday.

Roo won a cup. She was the Best Unknown Breed in her class. The judge said that he was not sure what type of dog Roo was, but he liked her anyway. Roo said her breed was famous for being unknown. She wanted to keep the cup in her

basket but I would not let her. It might get dented. We have to give it back next year.

You ask in your last letter if Roo and I will ever go on another adventure again. As a matter of fact, we have had numerous requests from complete strangers to lead expeditions all over the world. One of the letters was from a chap called Colonel Parker. He wanted Roo to lead an expedition up the Amazon in search of a lost city in the jungle. I had to write back and say that Roo is not good in jungles and that we had retired.

So for Roo and me the days of adventure are over. No more expeditions for us. Your mother would not allow it for a start. She says that we are both too old. I'm eighty this summer and Roo is not far behind. She's twelve, which is quite old for a dog. But she still chases rabbits when given the chance and she never lets the robin stay on the lawn. Roo still has a spring in her step and she loves life.

And rabbits. And digging holes.

And food. Which reminds me – I had better go

and feed her. Nothing comes between a dog and its
dinner.

with love Grandfather

P.S. I almost forgot. Uncle Freddie has invited us to
go down to Saltbottle for a few days. It's a lovely
little place by the sea. We are going to stay in a
hotel. Will write when we get there.

Waiting for dinner

The Seagull's Nest Hotel, Saltbottle

★ ★ ★ ★ ★

Guests are asked not to waste the writing paper
and to keep letters short and to the point.
Do not feed the gulls. Curfew by 8pm. Guests must
stay in their rooms after high tide.

Friday 2 September

Dear ~~Child~~.

Just a few lines to let you know that we are here.
The journey was awful.

Uncle Freddie drove us down. He's not that
keen on dogs and I think Roo sensed this. First of
all, he wanted Roo to go in a dog cage in the back.
Roo growled when she saw the cage and the idea
was quickly abandoned.

Roo went on the back seat in her basket
instead. There was a bit of an argument over
Poopy who had mysteriously appeared in the car.

I should say here
that Poopy is
a small grey
plastic walrus. He
honks in a most
annoying manner,

5

particularly when trodden on, which is often. Roo tends to leave him in the most awkward places. At the top of the stairs, for instance, or on the back doorstep. I have tripped over him many times and in truth am heartily sick of the little walrus.

But Roo adores him, so what can I do?

She would not give him back and slunk under the driver's seat with Poopy clenched in her mouth. Honking in that awful way of his. It was a dreadful start to our journey. I am afraid that in the end we had to give up and Poopy came on holiday with us.

We had not gone very far before Roo began playing us up. Said that she could not 'scent' properly in the back. Told her that we did not need her to 'scent' as we had a map, thank you.

Roo said that we were *bound* to get lost in that case.

Tried to ignore her.

Every five miles or so Roo would ask if we were there yet.

When I told her that we weren't, she would sigh dramatically and lie with her feet in the air making horrible choking sounds. Twice we pulled over to see what was wrong with her and each time she made a miraculous recovery and jumped in the front. When I tried to lift her back, she made herself heavy. It took both of us to budge her.

What with the honking, the skittering, the scrabbling and the snuffling, it all got too much for Uncle Freddie. He pulled over for lunch at a pub called the Dog and Goose and fled inside.

Roo was very interested when she saw the name of the pub – but no dogs were allowed in, I'm afraid. The landlord also told us that there was not, nor ever had been, roast goose on the menu and they did not want a dog to guard the pub from robins in return for scraps.

After lunch we got lost.

Roo was sitting on the map and Uncle Freddie missed the turning. It took us ages to find our way back on to the road to Saltbottle and we ended up in a place called Tarbucket.

Roo offered to scent but we did not need her help. I fell asleep and dreamt that Roo was driving the car. Woke up feeling quite unwell.

We eventually got to the Seagull's Nest at tea time.

The manager showed us to our room, which has a view of the kitchens. Never mind. Roo says that at least we will know what dinner is before anyone else. Uncle Freddie was disappointed to find that he was sharing the room with us. Roo was disappointed not to find any actual seagulls' nests in the hotel, despite keen searching under tables in the dining room.

The manager has asked me to keep her out of the dining room. As there have been complaints.

As I write this Roo is settled against my leg. She's had her own dinner and some of mine (she has decided that she is not keen on fish. Says it's for cats not dogs). But she's contented. So much so that she's gnawing her paw. Now she's laid her head on my knee. It really is nice to just get along. Like two peas in a pod. I'm so glad I have my dog with me.

Tomorrow we shall go to the beach and Roo will paddle and look for crabs.

with love from
your Grandfather

who did this?

The Seagull's Nest Hotel, Saltbottle

★★★★★

Guests are asked not to waste the writing paper and to keep letters short and to the point. Do not feed the gulls. Curfew by 8pm. Guests must stay in their rooms after high tide.

Saturday 3 September

Dear Child,

Having a lovely time.

Roo has just trotted in looking very pleased with herself. There is now a trail of muddy paw prints across the carpet. I would tell her off but she's still very sensitive about the cage incident.

Roo wants me to tell you that there are rabbits here at the Seagull's Nest but they are very, very small rabbits. (Not everyone is quite as interested in rabbits as you are, Roo.)

Sadly, Uncle Freddie has been called away on important business. When he was told that he could not have another room and would have to continue sharing with Roo and me, he looked very pale. At precisely that moment he went away to make a phone call and

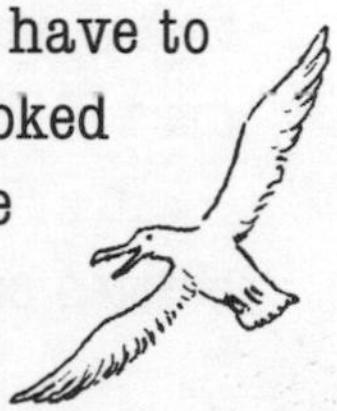

that's when he learnt he had to go away on urgent business to China. Something to do with tea, apparently. Anyway, it must have been urgent as he left in such a hurry that he forgot to take his golf bag and golf trolley with him. Uncle Freddie loves that golf trolley. It was designed by an astronaut, and has an onboard computer and an umbrella that automatically unfurls when it detects rain. We will look after it for him.

I hope that Uncle Freddie's departure has nothing to do with last night's misunderstanding.

Roo often gets into my bed in the middle of the night and I don't like it either. Roo says that the reason she savaged his hot-water bottle was because she thought it was a giant hairless rat trying to attack his feet. It gave Uncle Freddie a dreadful shock.

It's amazing what a bang those hot-water bottles can go off with.

Poor Uncle Freddie.

We're off to the beach now. Roo has discovered that bootlace seaweed can be dragged around to great effect. Yesterday she nearly cleared the beach entirely.

Here's the chambermaid to hoover the room. Best stop now.

Will write soon.

with love,

Grandfather

P.S. I had forgotten that Roo is not very good with vacuum cleaners. But I'm positive that it can be repaired, as she did a similar thing to mine.

The chambermaid was very understanding. She has a Yorkshire terrier that hates the telephone and won't go near one.

However, the manager was less understanding. He has just called to say that in future he will not take room service calls after midnight. And certainly not at three o'clock in the morning. Those twelve pizzas are going to have to be paid for.

I wish my dog hated the telephone.

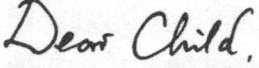

Sunday 4 September

LW 250
FOR SALE
The Girl Alison from Lerwick
In much better shape than the Unsinkable
Roo looking. I told her not to. But she did anyway.

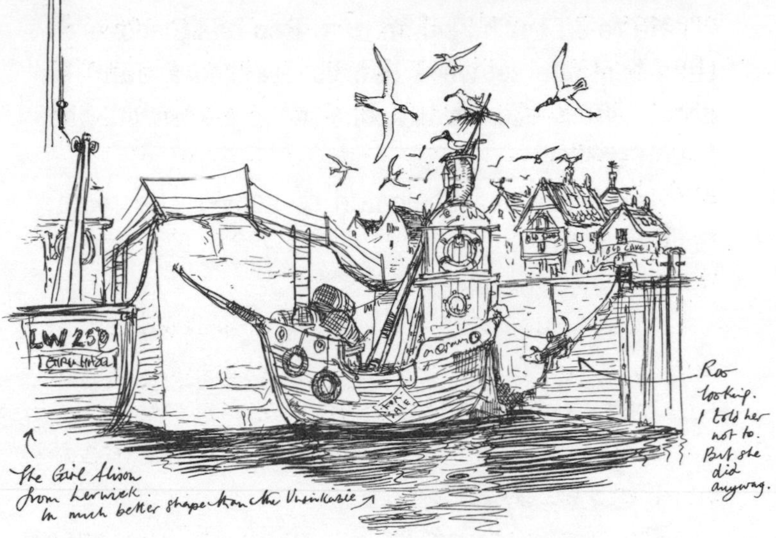

Dear Child,

An extraordinary thing has happened.

Do you remember when Roo and I went to the North Pole in search of polar bears? The ship we sailed on was called the *Unsinkable*. We sailed with the captain all the way up to the North Pole. We found the polar bears but got lost. Thankfully, the captain sailed back and found us. And saved our lives.

I often wondered what had happened to him and the *Unsinkable*. Was he still alive? Was the *Unsinkable* still afloat?

Today we made an amazing discovery.

We were strolling along the quayside eating ice creams and admiring all the old fishing boats in the harbour. I love looking at these old boats and like to imagine where they have been. They have such wonderful names like the *Lone Cormorant* and the *Ice Bear.*

Roo went down some very steep steps that were cut into the harbour wall.

I heard her barking at something. Tried to call her back but she pretended to be hard of hearing, which she has taken to doing recently.

In the end, I had to go down and take a look at what was upsetting her.

Roo was barking at an old boat. The boat looked in a sorry state. Barnacles grew all up her sides. Her hull was chipped and peeling. The mast was broken in the middle. A pair of herring gulls had nested in the funnel stack.

There was something familiar about the old wreck.

We had found the *Unsinkable*!

It was being sold today at noon and it was already a quarter to twelve! We rushed off to find the Sailor's Bunk as

quickly as we could.

(Dear, dear, it was so hard to find. Saltbottle has a maze of small lanes behind the harbour. We found it after Roo chased a cat into Fishgut Alley. An accident really and nothing to do with 'Cunning Instinct'.)

The Sailor's Bunk was a run-down hotel behind the gutting factory on Squab's Lane. There were some very unsavoury-looking characters in there and a strong smell of boiled cabbage and tobacco added to the atmosphere. We found the captain in the snug bar with his cronies.

He leapt to his feet when he saw us. Clasped Roo to his bosom and showered kisses on her. Hugged her to his chest and wept, afterwards wiping his nose on my sleeve. Said that Roo was the best sea dog a skipper could wish for. He was just telling everyone how Roo had once rebuilt the *Unsinkable*'s engine single-handedly (actually, she fell on it through an open hatch, an accident really, no skill involved at all) when the auction began.

A large crowd pressed noisily into the lounge bar. The captain fell back into my arms and sobbed loudly. Roo licked both our faces until I told her off. The captain gave her a packet of crisps and she took them under a table and tore them apart as noisily as she could (or so it seemed to me).

The auctioneer introduced himself by blowing his nose and hammering his gavel. He peered at us through a thick pair of bottle-end glasses and offered the *Unsinkable* for twenty pounds. There were no takers. The crowd coughed noisily, mainly in embarrassment for the captain. He sobbed louder into my ear.

The bidding eventually started. Rather ungenerously at five pounds. A scrap dealer called Foxy fought it out with a small chap in a tea-cosy hat called the Dickler. With the hammer poised at fifteen pounds, and the *Unsinkable* going to Foxy, the crowd gasped as a new bidder joined the sale, rapidly driving the bid up to a hundred pounds!

The auctioneer took his glasses off and bowed to the new bidder, called her Madam and blushed. I strained to see who the woman was but the crowd was restless and excited. I looked under the table. Roo had slipped away and was nowhere to be seen.

Jabbering numbers, the poor auctioneer barely had time to draw breath.

The bid rose dramatically to nine hundred and ninety-nine pounds and even I could see that the *Unsinkable* was not worth that sort of money.

But the captain was thrilled. He ordered another round of drinks for the whole house. Foxy was scratching his head, wondering how on earth he had found himself bidding so much for an old wreck. Exhausted, the auctioneer lay slouched over his lectern. His jacket had been discarded, his hat had fallen off and his glasses were steamed up. He raised his gavel for the last time. His voice was hoarse but just audible.

'Going once, going twice, going for the third and final time . . . Sold to the lady in the brown fur coat!'

The captain threw his hat in the air, kissed me on both cheeks and then collapsed on the floor. His friends carried him to the bar to revive him.

He seemed to have cheered up considerably.

Who was this mystery woman in the fur coat who had wasted her money on the *Unsinkable*? I craned with everybody else to see.

The crowd parted and the new owner was revealed.

Roo had bought the *Unsinkable*.

Afterwards, I had a dreadful row with the auctioneer, who explained that he could see *now* that Roo was a dog and not an old lady in a fur coat, but that his glasses had got steamed up during the sale. Still, the sale was binding. Had to write an IOU on the spot with Roo straining on her lead to get back to her crisps. The auctioneer said that we had twenty-eight days to pay up in full.

We found the captain in the bar celebrating with his chums. He said he always knew that the *Unsinkable* was a valuable ship. Had always said so. And that he would be proud to work under an owner like Roo and, what's more, he respected her and would fight any man who said that he didn't.

I'm afraid that we had a bit of a disagreement about the whole thing. In the end I stormed out, dragging Roo behind me on the lead (she wanted to stay and 'yarn with the boys').

Got the bus back to the hotel only to find the manager waiting for us. He did not look pleased. Our bags were packed and ready in the hallway with Uncle Freddie's golf trolley. The manager led me to the snooker room.

Across the snooker table, a trail of muddy paw prints criss-crossed the green baize. Roo said that she had thought it was an indoor lawn and that the pockets were rabbit holes. She did not know

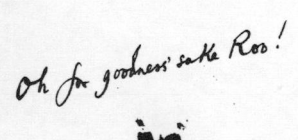

Oh for goodness' sake Roo!

18

where all the coloured eggs had come from. But guessed that they were probably from the Seagull's Nest.

After that the manager informed us that we were not the type of guests he wanted and showed us the door.

I am very cross with Roo, needless to say, and I'm worried about how we are going to pay for this wretched boat. It's a lot of money on a pension.

All the other hotels in Saltbottle were full up or did not take dogs. We were forced to return to the Sailor's Bunk. Technically, Roo, as the owner of the *Unsinkable*, is eligible for a cabin, whereas I, as a landlubber, qualify only for a hammock in the hallway. The porter signed me in grudgingly, saluted Captain Roo (as he insisted on calling her) and said that we would have to leave our seaboots outside our cabins. Really! We don't have any seaboots!

Don't tell your mother about all this. I'm sure it would just upset her. She was only saying last week how pleased she was that I had finally settled down. Don't worry. I will sort everything out and then come back home soon. Somehow or other we will raise the money for the *Unsinkable*.

with love Grandfather

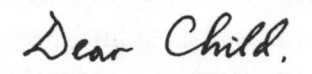

I am writing this letter to you from the Sailor's Bunk. The captain and his pals have been working on the *Unsinkable*, making her shipshape and ready for a fishing trip.

Our plan is very simple but brilliant. We are going to sail the *Unsinkable* to a place called the Door to the Sea, steam from there to the Forgotten Sea (see map), and after that navigate to the Great Cod Banks. If we are lucky, we will catch hundreds of codfish and when we get back to

Saltbottle, sell them and pay for the *Unsinkable*. The captain says that if we are extra lucky, we might even catch the King Cod himself. He is an extra-large codfish and might weigh as much as Roo (unlikely).

It's as simple as that. What can go wrong?

I have plenty of warm clothes and Roo is terribly excited to be going on a boat again. We will be back soon.

Much love,

Your Grandfather

P.S. Could you tell Uncle Freddie that his new golf trolley is still fine? Not a scratch on it. We've stowed it safely in the hold of the *Unsinkable*. Wretched thing keeps detecting rain and unfurling itself. I wish I could switch it off.

Bother!

The Log of the *Unsinkable*

Tuesday 6 September

Have decided to keep a diary or sea log of our fishing trip as I won't be able to send any letters when we are away. The captain says that when we get to the Great Cod Bank we will be too busy to sleep, let alone keep a log, but I'm going to try anyway.

Roo says she has decided to keep a log too. She found it on the beach yesterday. It's full of tiny crabs. And sea lice. And sand fleas. It will not be coming with us.

I threw it overboard when Roo wasn't looking. Was tempted to heave Poopy in after it but didn't.

Before we sailed, we stocked up on provisions at the Salty Grub, a sort of sailors' supermarket. I had to pay for all the provisions and I must say that I was very surprised at how much we had to

Roo's Log

take for a few days. There is enough here for a month at least. Surely Roo will not need all those tins of Mr Beefy Dogfood. But the captain said that sea air gives you a big appetite and that is why we need all this food. Roo pestered me to let her buy something and spent fifty pence on some quite useless articles. She bought: a can of ladies' fingers in brine, a get-well card with a silly rabbit on the front (who's ill?), and a sticky bun which she ate on the harbour wall, watched by two seagulls.

We left Saltbottle this evening.

There was a small crowd to see us off. The *Unsinkable* had been scrubbed and was looking quite smart. Her mast had been repaired, her hull repainted and varnished. Somebody had tied coloured lights to her mast.

The captain got carried away and showed off, firing a small cannon. A visiting yacht from the Isle of Wight had her mainsail holed.

We left hurriedly after that.

The captain navigated by using the Dog Star as his guide. It is his favourite star as it shines so brightly. Roo agreed it was hers too, for the same reason. Much better than the Cat Star, which she said was simply not to be trusted. I'd never heard of the Cat Star before. Roo agreed that it was not well known and spent most of its time hiding. We could not see it despite a long search.

Roo said that it was probably hiding behind the

moon. Playing with a ball of string. That made a lovely picture in my mind. Which Roo ruined by adding, either that or it had been run over and was lying flattened on a road like a dried-up pancake.

Sometimes she says the most awful things. It put me right off my supper. Pancakes and raspberry jam.

But Roo and the captain were very hungry. They ate a stack of pancakes.

Afterwards, whilst Roo lay under the table snoring, the captain told me more about the Forgotten Sea. Most fishermen didn't know where it was. All they had to do was find the Door to the Sea, sail through it and look for the Great Cod Banks. Then his eyes grew misty as he described the King Cod. How it had always been his ambition to catch it. It had been his father's ambition. Now it was his.

It's eleven o'clock as I write this. We are in our cabin. It is very cosy with the lantern and the stove on. Would not let Roo sleep in the hammock though. She's just not good in a hammock.

P.S. The captain keeps calling Roo 'Skipper' or 'Skip'. It is getting on my nerves. Roo knows nothing about boats. I will not be calling her 'Skip', that's for sure.
P.P.S. Poopy is getting on my nerves too. Conditions cramped at the best of times. Tripped over him twice today. I wish that Roo would not leave him on the galley steps. Somebody could get hurt.

It is not a good idea to
stand up in a hammock...

as the results ↑
can be distressing...

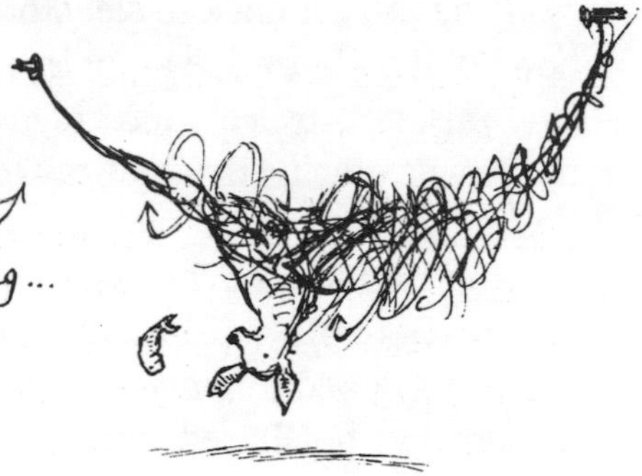

and difficult to untangle
afterwards.

What a terrible night.

I had just slipped off into a beautiful sleep when I was woken by Roo licking my face. It gave me quite a shock. She said that she was tired of being skipper of this boat and wanted to go back home, on the bus.

I explained to her why we couldn't, put her back in her basket and blew the lantern out. With great difficulty, got back up in my bunk.

I tried to get back to sleep but the *Unsinkable* was now rolling about like a pig in a poke. It was horrible. One minute my feet were higher than my head, the next I was staring down at my toes. I could hear Roo's basket sliding across the floor.

Roo abandoned her bed and scrambled up the ladder. Got into my bunk! When she stretched out, her paws poked into my ribs. These bunks were never designed to be shared with a dog.

The *Unsinkable* groaned and the engines laboured.

It was a dreadful night.

Neither of us could sleep. Roo whispered that if the bus wouldn't come, why couldn't Uncle Freddie fetch us in his car. I was too tired to explain again.

This is supposed to be Roo. Very hard to draw as the boat is going up and down ...

When I did drop off at last, I was woken once more by Roo.

She was worried that she did not know what a cod looked like. Her breed needs to know what they are looking for, otherwise they

can't hunt them properly. Explained
sleepily that a cod has a big mouth.
And jelly eyes. And a barb
on its chin.

The captain

this pen is useless!

After a long silence
Roo announced that
we should hunt for
chips instead. Told
her to go to sleep. In
an instant she was
snoring loudly in my ear.

I lay worrying about what would happen to us in
the Forgotten Sea. Would we catch any fish? Would
the captain catch the King Cod?

Nodded off at dawn to be woken a moment later
by the captain calling us to breakfast by banging on
the frying pan. Roo got up and yawned loudly in my
ear. Somebody had slept well at least.

The captain and Roo ate a huge breakfast
(sausages, beans, fried eggs, toast, porridge, hard-
boiled eggs, kippers, honey waffles, etc.). I had some
dry toast as I was not feeling well.

The boat is listing rather horribly.

There are too many captains on this ship and not
enough sailors. I am the only crewman. There's
nobody more junior than me aboard this boat.
Unless you count Poopy.

I am sick of being bossed around by a dog.
Roo has no idea how to sail a ship and I have no
confidence in her whatsoever.

She wanders all over the *Unsinkable*, sniffing into places that a dog should not. The engine room for instance. Or the bilges. Or the fish hold.

Poopy has to be taken everywhere, until Roo is interested in something else. Then she drops him. I seem to spend a lot of the day picking him up. My ankle is still sore from tripping on him the last time. He is a wretched nuisance. I don't care if he is 'bored'. He's a plastic walrus for goodness' sake!

And the captain has turned very bossy too.

He says that the last time I sailed with him I was a paying passenger and it was different. But now that I was crew, the shoe was on the other foot, so to speak. He made me scrub the decks this morning and afterwards came to inspect them. Pointed out a few bits that I had missed. Roo came along after him and pointed out a few more.

Mainly the dirty paw prints she'd left behind.

I am sick of it.

We have just passed a sea-bird colony. Gannets are my favourite birds. I could watch them for hours, diving into the sea. They drop from a great height, folding their wings at the last minute and then arrow into the water like darts.

The captain told me to stop gawking at the

I don't care if Poopy is 'bored'. He's a plastic walrus for goodness' sake!

28

gannets and get on with the
deck scrubbing.

Roo ate like a gannet
at lunch.

In fact, all she
thinks of at the
moment is food.

I wish the
captain would stop feeding her rich tea biscuits
under the table, or on it, for that matter. She is going
to be the size of a barrel at this rate.

I'm also getting a little tired of the captain and all
his bloodthirsty stories about the King Cod. How it
swallows ships and sailors in equal measures.

How it had hunted his father from Nantucket to
Colwyn Bay.

Dragging an oil rig behind it.

I don't believe a word of it.

The truth is we are not a happy ship.

I cheered up this evening, though, when we saw the whale.

What an amazing and beautiful creature. We heard
him before we saw him, singing his lonely whale song.
An eerie and mysterious music. Then we saw a plume
of water as he rose to the surface and blew.

It was a majestic sight and the captain said it was
a good omen for our trip.

I hope he's right.

We have made good progress today, so dinner was
taken early. The captain studied the sea charts. He
calculates sea miles by the length of his thumb (an

exact sea-mile long to scale) and uses his sea boot as a right angle. It is not an exact science but it seems to work for him. His stacked plate sat on the Great Cod Banks. A baked bean marked our position on the map. He was very hungry and eventually ate us too.

(Table manners seem to be deteriorating the further we get out to sea.)

Told Roo to get down off the table and not to lick our plates. The captain told *me* off for being so fussy. Then they both got on the table and licked the plates clean.

After I had washed up thoroughly, twice, the captain told us some more far-fetched stories. How when he was a boy and first went to the Cod Banks, the sea was so thick with cod that the ship almost ran aground. How he had been sent from one boat to another to get a pint of milk for the fisherman's tea. The cod were so tightly pressed together that he walked on their backs across the water.

Then the captain told us about the first time that he had ever seen the King Cod. His father had caught him and been towed all over the Forgotten Sea. Eventually the captain's father had given up after his boat had nearly sunk. After that, the captain said darkly, he swore that he would not rest until he had caught the King Cod. A wild look grew in his eye.

I'm not sure that we should be hunting the King Cod after all. He does not sound very nice. I was just about to say so when Roo rudely interrupted me

to
tell a story
about her Uncle Bob,
who she said had been a fisherman's dog.

I had never heard of Uncle Bob before and found the story very hard to believe. Something about how Uncle Bob could smell fish and used to stand on the prow of the boat sniffing for them. I don't see how a dog could smell under water but did not say so as the captain seemed very impressed and wondered if the skill had passed down to Roo.

Roo decided that it had.

She gave herself another rich tea biscuit as reward.

Left the captain and Roo talking about mermaids and mer-rabbits. I went to my bunk in a sulk.

Roo can sleep on the floor tonight in her basket. I nailed it to the floor so that it would not slide around.

The *Unsinkable* is pitching slightly as I write this in my bed. Roo has just barged in. It is almost eleven o'clock. Has got in her basket at last. Poopy greeted her with a raspy honk. She licked his head until she fell asleep. Well, almost.

Roo said sleepily that she will probably catch hundreds of chips tomorrow. Told her to go to sleep.

If she wakes me up tonight by getting into my bed, I will be cross.

where am I supposed to sleep?   Unused!

Thursday 8 September

Woken at six by the captain. He told me that we were near to the Door to the Sea. A thin rain was falling with a squally wind. It was hard to get out of my warm bed.

Roo was still fast asleep in her basket. As I was getting dressed, the captain came in to chivvy me along and said that he could sense that there were fish nearby. Said he could smell them. Roo woke up and said that she could smell them too.

She added that they didn't smell nice and went back under the covers. All I could smell was the *Unsinkable*. Diesel, stale fish and the captain's socks.

I wished we were at home.

I went up to see the Door to the Sea. Roo stayed in her basket. She said that she was tired of sea doors, cod banks and mer-rabbits. She said that her breed was only good on dry land after all. This voyage has left us both very jaded. We were not meant to go to sea.

But the Door to the Sea lifted my spirits again. I wish that Roo could have seen it rather than lying in bed. It would have cheered her too.

The Door to the Sea rose out of the waves to the height of St Paul's Cathedral. Gannets and kitty-wakes circled above it. Cormorants and shags stood on the turrets of rock and flapped their wings. The noise of the birds was ear-splitting.

Set in the rock was a great rusted door. It must have been over fifty metres tall. The captain pulled a buoy from the sea, in which was set a little lock. He took a small key from around his neck and inserted it. Then he cast the buoy back into the sea. The

huge rusted door groaned on its hinges and, driving a green wall of sea before it, began to open.

The captain set the *Unsinkable* to dead slow ahead. The great door groaned as it opened wider. Thousands of birds disturbed from their roosts took to the air. We sailed through on a great wave.

Then, as we sailed clear, the Door slammed shut behind us with a huge spume of spray.

We were in the Forgotten Sea.

The captain gave a great roar of joy.

Gannets wheeled above us and began diving on to the shoals of fish. The sea bubbled and I saw glints of silver as a huge shoal of sprat broke the surface of the sea. Behind them a great whale rose and spouted. The sprat rained down like stars into the sea. The seabirds dived on them. Then the whale dived deep and surfaced just beside us. I saw his small eye look over our tiny ship. Roo climbed out from the hatch and stood on the bowsprit, Poopy in her mouth. I'm not sure that she even noticed the whale, but I am certain that he saw her.

We sailed the Forgotten Sea all day long. How much life there is in this bit of the ocean. I saw the luminous plankton, curdling like cream across the water. Seals and walruses fed on the shoals of fish attracted to the plankton. The whale sang his lonely song over and over again. What a beautiful ocean this is.

Then, in the afternoon, we came to an area of sea that the captain said was special. It looked like all the

rest to me. But the captain had a feeling about
this bit and swore that it was the same bit of
sea that his father had shown him as a boy.

This is where the King Cod lives.

We began fishing. With the net out behind us, we
trawled round and round in little circles. Partly
because that is what the captain wanted. But mostly
because that is how Roo always steers.

Must stop writing now as we are going to haul the
nets in. All hands on deck!

Hurrah! We did not catch the King Cod.

But we have
caught lots of fish!
Codlings and big
fat haddocks. The
deck was flowing
with them.

We filled the fish
boxes and stacked
them on the deck. The
Unsinkable is so laden
with fish that she sits
heavy in the water. We
were followed by a
flock of seagulls
attracted by our
catch. The captain
threw them
fish guts.
Roo looked

on enviously, until she tried some for herself. After that her envy disappeared fast. She went looking for sausages instead.

Sat under the fridge looking mournful as there aren't any.

Never mind, Roo. Soon we will be back home and there will be lots of sausages for you!

We are sailing home. The expedition has been a success.

The captain has already calculated that we will be able to pay for the *Unsinkable* four times over and still have enough left for a holiday.

Why he has to drink so much grog now, I do not know.

I am going to bed to read my book that I bought for the holiday. I have not had time to read it as we have been so busy. It is a wonderful book called *Robinson Crusoe*. Hopefully, by the time I have finished it, we will be home.

Roo has just come in and asked me where Poopy is. How am I to know?

I'm going to get some sleep now.

Friday 9 September

Disaster! The *Unsinkable* is sinking.

We are taking on a lot of water. It's all Roo's fault. The captain has said that now is not the time for blame. But I feel I must record for the log the true events of last night.

<u>Ten reasons why Roo is guilty as charged</u>

1. Roo found Poopy on deck with the fish. Annoyed and glad to see him safe, she gave him a severe chewing. His honks attracted several large seagulls. A fight with them caused the *Unsinkable* to shift into reverse gear.

2. The *Unsinkable* backed up to a small flat rock. A colony of seals awoke and came to see what all the fuss was about. They found a fishy midnight feast 'at their door', so to speak.

3. The *Unsinkable* was very low in the water due to the large catch. The seals got on board very easily and made it lower in the water. They are not responsible for the actual cause of the ramming, however.

4. That rests with the whale.

5. Who confused Poopy's honk with the lovesick song of the female humpback whale. A combination of his humpback and his ardour for Poopy caused notable damage to the bows. But not the actual sinking.

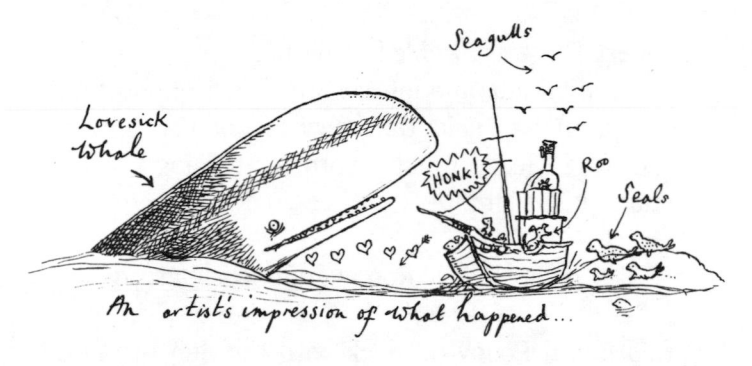

An artist's impression of what happened...

6. That remains with Roo.

7. Who did not wake the captain.

8. Or me.

9. But chose foolishly instead.

10. To throw the *Unsinkable* into top gear, sail in a wide circle and bash Seal Island a second time. We

were woken by the bang. Thrown headfirst out of bed actually.

Now the *Unsinkable* is lying stricken just to the north of Seal Island.

Her engines are making a terrible noise and there is a nasty smell of burning oil and diesel. The water is rising in the bilges. We fall to the pumps and keep pumping all night.

We are slowly sinking. The thing is not to panic. We bail out water but it keeps coming in as fast as we pump it out.

ABANDON SHIP!

We are cold and tired. Roo shivers on the deck fast flooding with water. Fish boxes float off into the cold sea. The captain splashes around doing his best to save the *Unsinkable*. But it is a losing battle that he cannot win.

The *Unsinkable* has been mortally wounded.

The captain hauls out the lifeboat and sets it in the water. He rescues food and provisions from below.

41

With the golf trolley, he stacks it all into the stern of the lifeboat, which I notice is called the *Little Pig*.

Next, he lifts Roo and me over the side into the little boat. Wraps us up in warm blankets and wedges us under the awning. We are too cold to resist. Slowly he pushes us away from the *Unsinkable* with a boat hook.

We beg him to join us in the lifeboat but he will not come. He waves to me and salutes Roo.

The last we see of him, he is standing behind the wheel.

We drift slowly away.

The sea carries us where it will.

A purple flare rises from the *Unsinkable* and lights up the sky.

It falls back down in the inky night. The darkness returns. I hear the *Unsinkable*'s foghorn call out once more in the darkness.

But no answer comes back.

Nothing but the wind on the waves.

Then a great star falls from the sky and the night swallows the *Unsinkable* up and we see her no more.

Saturday 10 September

No land in sight. Roo wants to know where the captain is. Cannot tell her. Told her that he had gone to get help. Roo said that he had probably gone home on the bus. Must conserve energy. No land, no ships. Nothing.

Sunday 11 September

Still no sign of land.

Monday 12 September

Raining. We are snug under the awning at least. The rain drips off the awning into Roo's dog bowl. We are taking turns to drink from it as it is the only drinking bowl we have. Though I still cannot get used to drinking out of a dog bowl. Roo says that's what it's like for her when she has to eat off my plate. Ignored her. Must keep spirits high and not be drawn into pointless arguments.

Bad news.

We are being followed by a shark.

Saw its fin cutting through the water and then it swam round and round our little boat examining us.

Tuesday 13 September

Tonight the shark has been back.

Roo wanted to fight it. Had to put her on her lead to stop her leaping into the sea after it.

She is brave but reckless. Keeping tight grip on lead through the night.

Wednesday 14 September

A squally wind blustered across the waves and with it came a shoal of flying fish. Roo was confused by the flying fish. Wanted to chase them across the waves. Good thing she was on the lead. Luckily one landed in our boat and we had it fried in the pan in no time.

Roo enjoyed it. But I think that she would eat anything at the moment. Caught her looking at my shoes this evening. I'm sure that I heard her say something like Good Meat to herself. But I may have dreamt it. No sign of the shark. Maybe he has tired of us.

Thursday 15 September

Very weak.

The flying fish did not agree with me. Feeling rather poorly.

Roo has been looking at me in a very odd way all day long.

Almost wolfish.

I wish she would stop it.

The wind died away in the afternoon and we drifted aimlessly in small circles. Too tired to row. Big dark clouds started gathering in the afternoon.

We are lashing down the tarpaulin.

Shared out rations in the half light of the lantern. Lamp fuel running low.

In the half light Roo looked more wolfish than usual.

Friday 16 September

A terrible storm. The waves are lashing at the *Little Pig* angrily. My dog and I are together under the awning. It's all that matters. Can write no more.

This Log was found in the sea by
Arthur C. Lyons (9) on Yellow Craig's Beach,
nr North Berwick.

Saturday 17 September

My dear Child,

How we survived that storm I will never know. We saw waves as big as houses. Sometimes we were in the valleys of these waves, and sometimes on the very crests. It was a horrible night.

The wind battered our little boat and tossed us about like a paper kite. Roo and I huddled together under the leaking tarpaulin, and slept on her basket under the eiderdown. We prayed for the morning to come soon. We fell asleep and dreamt restless dreams as golfballs rolled around in the waterlogged hull of the *Little Pig*.

In the morning we were woken by the sweetest sound.

Waves crashing on a shore.

Land!

I whooped with joy and started to row towards the shore.

But it was a dangerous ride through the coral reef that protected the island. The *Little Pig*'s hull was scoured and cut by the sharp coral under our keel. It scraped a hole in no time and the water began to flood in. Soon it was up to our ankles.

We were sinking again.

Suddenly the shark's fin cut the water. Behind us. Only metres away. I armed myself with the oar and waited for the shark to attack. Just as he closed in on us with his great toothy mouth gaping, the golf-trolley umbrella unfurled.

A strong gust of wind caught the umbrella and dragged us off the reef and away from the shark. We sailed up above the waves, articles of clothing and golf balls falling below us.

Hanging on to the trolley like windsurfers, we skimmed across the water. We glided safely on to the beach, the wheels of the trolley making a

perfect touchdown.
I lay in the sand
and thanked our
lucky stars that
we had made
it. Roo went
up the beach as
if she did this sort of thing
all the time.

This bird is Roo's enemy...
(Actual size)

* Twitus Minimus or Lesser Twit

She chased a small bird down the beach and lay under a palm tree and went to sleep.

We are marooned on what we have called Roo's Island. Perhaps we shouldn't have called it that as it might belong to somebody else. But as far as I can tell we are the only people here.

We explored our beach and although we have not been into the jungle yet, the chances of finding another human being are very slim.

Roo and I are very wobbly from all our time in the *Little Pig*. The land sometimes feels like the sea. We ride imaginary waves in our sleep. Our dreams are fitful and restless. Sometimes I hear Roo cry out. I hope that she is chasing dream rabbits and is not afraid.

Oh, why was I so foolish as to believe that we could go to sea? It has cost us dearly, this senseless journey.

If we are to be saved, we must to do it our-
selves. Told Roo and she said that as far as she
was concerned it was every dog for herself, which
is very selfish and not the spirit I was looking for.
It is teamwork that will get us off this island. Told
this to Roo and she said that she wanted to be in
my team, which was good. But she said she
would leave the work to me, which wasn't.

She did not help me with building the shelter.

She lay in the shade of the golf trolley and
gnawed her paws instead. Said that dogs can

survive outdoors and don't need homes. I ignored
her and got on with building a rough hut.

Here are all the things that I have been able to
salvage from our shipwreck: the golf trolley, Roo's
basket, her dog eiderdown, a box of Mr Beefy dog-

food, two packets of Snacksticks, one red bowl (Roo's), a pen, a bottle of ink, a fishing hook and some line, a kettle, thirty teabags, a tin opener, a kerosene lantern, some oil, a penknife (very useful) and lastly Poopy (not so useful).

The *Little Pig* is beyond repair though. I doubt that it will ever get us off this island. It floated in today and promptly collapsed on the beach. We salvaged it (well, me mainly as Roo did not help).

I used the prow of the *Little Pig* and an old piece of corrugated iron for a roof. Our shack is built between two palm trees. It's the best I can do with what we have.

I've done a drawing of it for you. You see the gramophone player? Roo found that on the beach. It's in perfect working order. I wish we had some records to play. Wouldn't that be lovely? I miss music so much.

Roo says that she misses rabbits more. It's not a competition, Roo.

It is raining as I write this. The rain is lashing down on the roof. At least we are dry.

I found a book washed up on the beach today. It was very wet but I dried it over the fire. It turned out to be a blank diary. It is called 'A Victorian Lady's Good Deed Diary' and it has weights and measures, full moon timetables and wise sayings at the top of each day. I shall record our times here in it.

I miss the captain tonight. Roo is not concerned about him. Said that the *Unsinkable* was called Unsinkable because it was unsinkable. The captain would come for his dinner soon, she said.

I'm afraid that my explanation of why something being *called* something doesn't mean it *is* something fell on deaf ears. Roo just does not understand our plight.

She thinks that we are on holiday as we spend most of the day on the beach. Wants to know why she can't have an ice cream. Sits and waits under the coconut tree for the bus to come and take us back to our hotel. How can I tell her that it will never arrive?

We must keep our spirits up.

Roo found this plastic shampoo bottle on the beach. I am putting this letter inside it. I shall throw it in the sea and hope that one day it finds you.

with love,
Grandfather.

An Account of Life on
a Desert Island with a Dog

Sunday 18 September
The early bird catches the worm. Full Moon.

How true!

We are not on holiday, despite what Roo thinks.

This crab cannot read.

We are trying to get off this island.

Roo got up around noon and chased a small bird off the beach. Then she lay under a palm tree and searched in her tail. I gathered wood for tonight's fire whilst Roo buried a reluctant and very much alive crab in the sand.

I have been reading to Roo from the book I managed to stash away before the shipwreck. Roo was not taken as I was by the coincidence that we, like the author, are shipwrecked and marooned on a desert island. Said it was his own fault for not going home on the bus. But she liked his dog and said that he reminded her of her.

Robinson Crusoe's dog is actually very helpful and is nothing like Roo. There is no mention of him digging holes in the camp or pointlessly

Robinson Crusoe's dog

chasing small birds off the beach. He helped his master in all sorts of useful ways. Like hunting pigs and rounding up wild goats.

Roo said that she would round up goats when given the chance. Then she fell asleep on my bed.

Wednesday 21 September
Neither a borrower nor a lender be.

It has rained for three days on the trot and we are both thoroughly miserable. The roof leaks. Roo's criticism was not helpful. I did not bother

Waiting for the Rain to stop

explaining why we could *not* get a proper builder to make a real roof. I patched it up as best I could with what came to hand.

Roo no help at all. Either sleeping in the shack. Or digging a hole in it. The floor by the cooking area is littered with small scraps. A rabbit makes less mess.

A large puddle of rain has grown by the door. It threatens to come inside.

We are fed up.

How I wish this rain would stop.

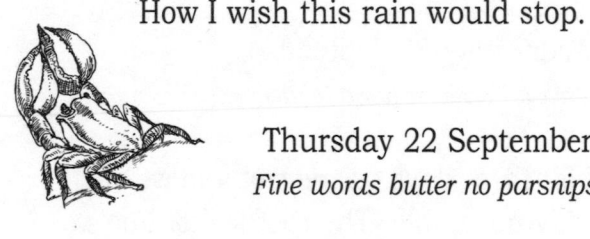

Thursday 22 September
Fine words butter no parsnips.

It has stopped raining at last and has now grown very hot. Insects chatter in the trees. The sun scorches the beach. The muddy patch that grew at the door has dried up at last. The sun sent Roo into a flurry of activity. She buried another reluctant crab on the beach. Then chased a small crab under the shack and spent all morning trying to dig it out. There was a big hole growing at the back and the shack was creaking dangerously.

I was cleaning the dog bowl down in the sea when I heard it fall over.

Oblivious, Roo trotted off to find something else to wreck.

Did Robinson Crusoe's dog behave like this? I don't think so.

Rebuilt the shack alone.

Friday 23 September

*Hang out your washing on
a cucumber wind.*

It has been even hotter today.

Have made myself a drinking bowl out of a coconut shell to save myself using the dog bowl any more. Roo said that she was relieved to have her bowl to herself again. She bolted her dinner down very quickly and went off to hunt crabs.

Told her to stay away from the shack. I'm sick of rebuilding it every day.

I followed her along the beach to see what she was doing but I lost sight of her in the thick leaves.

I called and whistled for her but she did not come back. Followed a little path where I thought she had gone in and was amazed to find myself in a clearing surrounded by the most beautiful fruit trees.

Mango, passionfruit, ripe bananas and even some fruit that I have not encountered before. One was shaped like a trumpet and tasted like strawberries. The other was in a thick spiky skin that when peeled revealed a chocolate-flavoured nut. Delicious!

Roo came back very excited and said that she had chased a little horse down a rabbit hole. Her imagination has remained intact at least.

We will not starve.

There is plenty of fruit here. The only thing we are running low on is dog food. Roo has been doubling her own ration. When we run out, I don't know what we will do.

To keep our spirits up I have organized a few games on the beach. Sadly, with little success. Roo tends to forget that we are playing cricket or catch; she finds little crab holes far more interesting. Fortunately, her distractions proved fruitful today.

She found a box on the beach. It was covered in barnacles and must have been in the sea for a very long time. But inside, in admirable condition, were three records.

Swan Lake, Snowflakes Are Dancing, and a record by a group called the Mouse Family. We

ran back to the
gramophone and
put on *Snowflakes
Are Dancing*. It
was wonderful to
hear music again.
We played the
records over and
over as the sun
set and our fire roared. Some seals came
to listen to the music.

Like Roo, their favourite was the Mouse
Family.

The Mouse Family is a family of singing mice
who harmonize in high-pitched voices. They can
really get on your nerves after a while.

Little brown dogs and seals adore them,
though.

Some of the mouse songs were quite sad, it
has to be said. The one about the cowboy mouse
who meets his fate in a mousetrap disguised as a
saloon was particularly moving. 'Stand By Your
Mouse' was the most popular song. The seals
joined in with husky tenors on the chorus while
Poopy honked the whole song.

A dreadful racket ensued.

I was glad when the sunset came at last and

we all went to bed.

I was tempted to throw the record back into the sea, but Roo had taken it to her basket.

Sunday 25 September

Children (and small dogs)
should be seen and not heard.

Woken by the Mouse Family. Will try and hide the winding key for the gramophone after breakfast. Can't be woken by that every morning.

Have been notching the days that we have been here (nine) on a tree beside our camp. Roo watched me. Uninterested.

Said that she wanted to know when we were

Roo thinks that the Mouse Family live in here!

going home.

Said that she was tired of waiting for the bus.

Wanted to use the telephone.

To call her friend Muffin, a bearded collie.

Whose mum has a car.

That could come and get us.

It took a lot of explaining to her that we couldn't and it put me in a grumpy mood.

I played golf alone on the beach. Then the rain came and spoilt it. Dark clouds were rolling in from the sea.

Retreated back to camp. Wretched umbrella automatically detecting rain only after I had been soaked to the skin.

At least the new roof is keeping us warm and dry. Put the kettle on the fire and made a cup of tea. Only two tea bags left now. I wish we had a tea bag tree. That would be nice.

Roo is lying in the doorway, her head between her paws. Watching two crabs play tig on the beach with their claws raised up. A little bird flew down and had a quick bath in Roo's bowl. Even this did not arouse her interest.

Spirits very low at teatime. My clothes are beginning to fall apart. I have made myself a hat from a plastic vegetable strainer I found on the beach. Threaded with palm leaves and some feathers, it keeps the sun off. A piece of rope holds my frayed trousers up.

Monday 26 September

'Be kind to little creatures,
Whatever they may be,
And if you see a starfish, why,
Shove it in the sea.'

How odd.

This afternoon a hot wind came blowing in from the sea. The insects awoke in the trees and began their whirring songs, drumming on shell case and thorax, wings beating on armoured legs, rattling, clattering, to an unseen insect conductor up in the trees. Roo started barking and soon she was joined by other creatures who lent their voices to the song. The wind howled and moaned softly in the palm trees. Even the mosquitoes stopped their search for blood, blown by that torrid wind. Softly, the insects began with a new song. A last trill from those rattling legs and then silence.

In the evening dozens of pink starfish lay on the beach. I slipped them back into the sea again.

I have decided to build a raft. Then we will sail back to you.

I wish I had some tools.

I must think.

Tuesday 27 September
Wake not a sleeping wolf.

As I write this the waves are breaking on the coral reef. It is a pleasant sound. Roo is asleep beside me in the shack, snoring softly. She's had a busy day today.

We were just looking for some bits of wood to make our raft when we made an important discovery.

We are not alone!

Roo found the footprint. It is most definitely

human. And it wasn't mine.

You can imagine our joy. We must have looked a strange sight. The two of us leaping around in the sand throwing seaweed up in the air. Roo thought that it was a great game.

Judging from the footprint, the person must have walked right past our camp. Barefoot. It would be good to see another human face.

Roo agreed that it would. Said that she was tired of looking at mine every day.

The feeling is mutual, I told her.

Woken after lunch by fierce barking.

Roo was chasing something or somebody down the beach. There was a familiar honk, a muffled cry and then a heavy thud.

Poopy had claimed another victim.

Poopy's victim was an old man with a straggly beard. He looked extremely undernourished and he had twisted his ankle. Poopy lay with a vacant smile in the sand. I resolved to have him court-martialled in the morning.

Helped the castaway up the beach to the shack. He was wearing a dressing gown and a pair of bright-red shorts. He had probably grabbed whatever came to hand when he was shipwrecked. He had dropped a towel further up the beach.

Back at the camp under the kerosene lamp, I tried to communicate with him.

He does speak. But in a strange, made-up gobledegook. His beard muffles most of his words. He mumbled something unintelligible.

He seemed afraid of me and would not drink the tea from Roo's bowl. Kept pushing it away with a feeble hand. Maybe he has a fever. They say that you should feed a fever and starve a cold. Or is it the other way around? Anyway, I decided that he could do with a good feed. Roo agreed to open the tin of ladies' fingers that she had been saving for a special occasion.

'Ladies' fingers in brine,' I yelled at him.

Maybe he was put off by Roo, who said that she did not like the lady's fingers and spat them out on the floor.

HONK!

The same thing will happen again if Roo is not careful.

The poor castaway muttered something about cannonballs. I think he has been dreadfully traumatized.

But it is so good to have human company again!

Wednesday 28 September
Beginning of 'Be Nice to Elk' Season.

I made him as comfortable as I could. He cannot lie in my hammock because of his ankle. But the poor chap would not really settle in Roo's basket. It didn't help that Roo kept getting in it with him. Said that a dog's saliva can heal anything, even a twisted ankle. Told her not to as it was obvious that he didn't like having his feet licked.

Perhaps that's why he got up several times in the night and tried to crawl out of the shack. It took a lot of effort to get him back in again. Perhaps he has been out in the sun too long. Must have wandered to our camp in his delirium. Thank goodness we found him.

He looked very nervous when I showed him Uncle Freddie's golf clubs. But he is obviously not a golfer and seemed afraid of them, particularly the driver for some reason. When I tried to show him where I was going wrong with my drive, the poor chap scuttled under the table. Poor old fellow.

I wonder what horrors he has endured. Here. Alone on the island. For all these years . . .

We will get him better though.

It was nice of Roo to play him the Mouse Family. He came out from under the table and listened, with what looked like a smile. The Mouse Family has that effect it seems.

Thursday 29 September
End of 'Be Nice to Elk' Season.

The poor castaway is a little better this morning. Roo watched him eat out of her bowl a little too closely. I hate it when she does that. The castaway seemed very hungry. Hunched over the bowl and growled. Roo growled back.

Perhaps he was a sailor like we were. This morning I tried to ask him where his boat had sunk. But he did not point to the wide blue sea as I had expected, but pointed up to the jungle instead and said something like 'Ho Tell'. Over

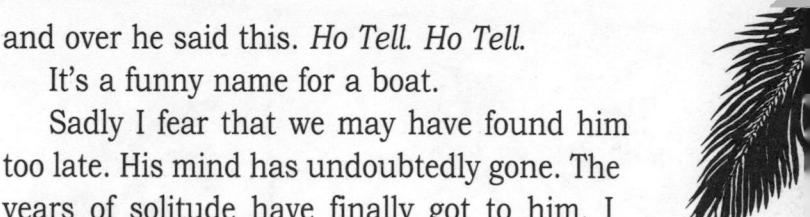

and over he said this. *Ho Tell. Ho Tell.*

It's a funny name for a boat.

Sadly I fear that we may have found him too late. His mind has undoubtedly gone. The years of solitude have finally got to him. I fear that Roo and I may soon share the same fate. Roo possibly quicker than me, though.

I have decided to call the castaway Tuesday, as that was when we found him. Roo's suggestion that we call him Weekly was ignored.

Poor old Tuesday.

He mopes around the camp on his new crutches. But we will need the oars back once we have built the raft. Hopefully he will be fit soon and able to row.

Tried to get him to help us with the raft. But he was about as much use as Roo has been. Pointing into the jungle and going on about his boat, the *Ho Tell.* Tried to make him understand that our boats lie on the bottom of the sea and that this raft is the only way that we will get off this island. He looked very despondent after that. I helped him back up to the shack. His ankle is still very swollen.

Poor old Tuesday. We must save him and take him away with us. Even if we have to bind him hand and foot.

A lonely hermit crab

It's for his own good.

All evening Tuesday has been restless.

He refused the boiled banana soup I made him.
Angrily pointing to the jungle. Jabbering words that
I did not understand. Probably the weird
gobbledegook that he had learnt in his seclusion.
From what I could make out by the tone of his voice,
I pictured that before he had met us his life had
been pretty awful on the island. Lost in the jungle.
Perhaps sheltering in a dismal cave. Eating worms
and grubs. Clawing at the dark earth for roots to
gnaw upon. I shuddered. In his dressing gown,
Tuesday sat in Roo's basket and glared at me.

Then Roo told a highly irrelevant story about
her Uncle Bob, who sounds, I must add, like a bit
of a bore.

How Uncle Bob had once lived in a hotel. He got to eat the guests' breakfast when they couldn't finish them, and how, in order to hasten the chances of this happening, he used to lie under their tables and make wind.

Well, that's not exactly how Roo put it, but for the purposes of the log I need not dwell on the details of the story. Like how he fanned it with his tail, etc., etc.

Suffice to say that the story lingered around afterwards and neither Tuesday nor I felt hungry after that. Roo finished both our dinners.

 ### Friday 30 September
Every dog has his day.

Tuesday has been showing the effects of his years as a wild man. Last night he tried to escape and return to his cave. Had to stop him from trying by tying him up with Roo's lead. The good news is that my efforts to teach him English are working. This morning he wrote

71

FILM DIRECTOR CAPTURED BY PIRATES
'My hell with wild man and wolf creature...'

The world-famous film director Marshall L. Marshall was recovering last night from his ordeal after being captured by a gang of pirates on the luxury resort of St Kitty's Island.

Mr Marshall had got lost in the grounds of the luxury hotel and stumbled upon the makeshift camp that the pirates had erected on the beach. Wrestled to the ground by a wolf creature, and mauled by a third pirate called Mr Poop (never captured and believed to be still at large on the island), the American director was forced to live in a low hovel built on the beach.

Threatened with a golf club and kept in a dog basket, the director tried to escape many times. During the hottest hours of the day, he was ordered to work on a heap of logs on the beach.

When the coastguards found him, the pirates were just

Marshall L. Marshall (73)

about to put to sea on this pile of logs. Mr Marshall was attached by a dog lead to a golf trolley on top of these logs.

The wild man and his dog were taken to the island gaol where they were bailed out by a rather rich gentleman calling himself the captain of the redoubtable *Unsinkable* (proven).

Asked to describe his ordeal last night, the elderly director shuddered and said, 'They made me eat out of a dog bowl.'

Mr Marshall is 73.

Dear Child,

We have been saved! Roo wants me to send you this news clipping.

I cannot describe how wonderful it was to see the captain again. There was a lot of hugging and tears and Roo licked his face until it shone. Then the captain explained to the coastguards and the police how we were really heroes after all and how the *Unsinkable* had nearly been sunk by a whale (he winked at Roo when he said this) and then he told us all the most amazing story that even Roo could not better.

After he fired the last purple rescue flare and the *Unsinkable* was going down slowly, he decided  to have one last go at catching the King Cod. He baited a hook with the last thing he had, one of his boots, and started fishing. He had

only been trying for about five minutes when the rod nearly bent in two. He had hooked the King Cod, the biggest fish in the world. The captain lashed himself to the *Unsinkable* and held on grimly. The King Cod began to drag the *Unsinkable* this way and that. The captain hung on for dear life. The King Cod jumped out of the water, it dived deep, but still the captain hung on. It dragged the *Unsinkable* around all night, until at last it was beaten. It beached itself in the shallows of a small island. The *Unsinkable* ran aground on the beach.

But the captain is not a cruel man. When he

saw the great fish dying in the shallows he felt sorry for the King Cod and decided to save its life. He unhooked the great fish and pushed it back into the deeper waters. The King Cod recovered and swam off.

It was only when the captain had been on the island for many days that he made a wonderful discovery. For the island had been the hiding place of a real pirate and he had buried his treasure under the two palm trees. In an old chest, heaps of golden coins and precious jewels were stacked.

Loading the treasure on to the *Unsinkable*, the captain had managed to sail away from the island on a high tide. One night he stumbled across St Kitty's, and when he heard about the wild man and his dog he knew that it was us. He has not let us out of his sight ever since.

Marshall L. Marshall, the film director, has been most kind. He realizes now that *he* saved *us*. He wants to make a film about the whole thing and he's thinking of calling it *The Mystery of Roo Island*. Would like Roo to play herself. Roo agreed that nobody else could do it better. Apart from Tom Cruise.

Mr Marshall bought her an ice cream to seal the deal in the Ice Cream Snooker Bar.

They think of everything here at St Kitty's.

Roo does not know that this island is called St Kitty's. I'm sure it would horrify her if she did. On Marshall L. Marshall's insistence, all signs have been covered that show the name. Instead, a few hastily contrived notices keep her oblivious. This is still Roo's Island as far as Roo is concerned. Not that she has been busy patrolling the luxury beach here. She is too busy checking all the snooker tables for little rabbits.

Roo says that next year she wants to go on holiday in a caravan. They are like a home but they have wheels. Roo reckons that if your home is on wheels you can always take it with you. Dogs are good in caravans apparently, she says.

I will not take her word for it.

with love from
your Grandfather

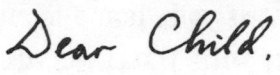

Dear Child,

We left St Kitty's in the repaired and newly furnished *Unsinkable* yesterday. The captain has spared nothing on the old ship and, though I am impressed by the new luxurious cabins and fabulous fitted kitchen, I find some bits of the boat a little ostentatious actually. Is there really a need for the captain and Roo to have their names emblazoned all over the wheel house like that? And those matching thrones for Roo and the captain? But it's the captain's money, I suppose, and he can do what he wants with it.

We were quite sad to say goodbye to the little beach where we had spent so much time. We sailed past it and I was cheered to see that the little shack was still standing. The last we saw of it over the blue waves was the fringe of white sand and our gramophone. Just as we were leaving we saw Marshall L. Marshall waving. I heard the faint sounds of the Mouse Family come across the water.

We sailed away until soon St Kitty's was just a speck on the horizon. We never saw the King Cod, nor Roo's whale either, but as we sailed

WELCOME BACK   WELCOME BACK

through
the Door to the Sea, the gannets
dived and wheeled about us for the last time. We
sailed south through sleepy waters back to
Saltbottle. Roo slept well in her specially designed
dog hammock. A good night's sleep was had by all.

The next morning a large flotilla of boats of all
descriptions was there to lead us into Saltbottle.
The captain had radioed to let them know we were
coming. He let Roo bark into the walkie-talkie.
They both enjoyed her doing that until I told her to
stop it.

Saltbottle was decorated with flags and
bunting when we arrived. A large crowd cheered
as the *Unsinkable* finally touched the safety of the
harbour wall. We were home! The band played
'Waltzing Matilda' and everybody sang. It was the
most moving occasion.

Afterwards, the captain said that he was going
to miss us and I thought that he was going to cry.
Then he got a strange look in his eyes and for a
moment I thought he wanted us to go back to sea
with him. But instead he muttered something
about caravans. Then he rushed off to the Sailor's
Bunk to make a phone call. Roo went with him.

It's all very mysterious.

They are still not back, Child, as I write this letter to you. I hope that they won't be too late. I wonder what they are doing?

with my love,
Grandfather.

Dear Child,

This is my last letter to you for a while. Our adventure is over. Mind you, you never know with Roo. Adventures just seem to happen to her. Roo agreed that her breed was renowned for it.

Which I suppose must be true.

Which brings me to what Roo did next. Her idea about a caravan holiday had inspired the captain. When they got back last night, they were very excited. They had an enormous crane with them. The *Unsinkable* was lifted out of the water and put on the back of a trailer. A big red lorry was there to

tow it. We got in the lorry with the captain and he drove out of Saltbottle, towing the *Unsinkable* behind.

As I write this last letter to you, we are driving along a calm and even road. The high tides are carrying us back home. The captain is a good driver. We're nearly there now.

Roo is snuggled up next to me. Shall we close our eyes and sleep a little?

When we awake, the captain is reversing the trailer into our garden.

The captain unhitches the *Unsinkable*. It looks very nice there by the pond. He's going to stay for a little while. No doubt in the spring he will be off again. But for the winter he will stay with us. Roo says it will come in handy having him so close. She pops up the ladder for one last rich tea biscuit. The captain gives it to her and pats her on the head.

Good dog, Roo!

We wave goodnight to our new neighbour and go back along the garden path to our house.

Come inside and let's get warm by a big fire, Roo. Yes, tonight we *are* having sausages. But no starfish. When have I ever given you starfish?

Come on, Roo. The robin has gone to bed too. He's not under that milk bottle. Don't forget to bring Poopy with you. Where is he? How should I know? The last I saw of him he was hiding down there. Let's have a look.

I can't see a thing.

Honk!

Oooww!

I told you not to leave him there.

Never mind.

It didn't really hurt that time.

Yes, you are still my best friend.

Yes, I would go anywhere with you.

Yes, I would.

My dog, Roo.

Just me and you.

<u>Author's Apology:</u>

For the purposes of this novel some names have been changed
to protect the innocent.

The captain of the Unsinkable bears <u>no</u> relation to
Captain Fred McBroom, skipper of the Gannet, Lerwick, Shetland.

Poopy bears a passing resemblance to Squeaky, a small plastic
walrus, but that is by accident, and no disrepect is intended.

The Seagull's Nest Hotel is taking bookings (no dogs) now.